Stage Fright
by Edgar J. Hyde

Illustrations by Chloe Tyler

PAB-0608-0301 • ISBN: 978-1-4867-1877-1

Copyright ©2020 Flowerpot Press, a Division of Flowerpot Children's Press, Inc., Oakville, ON, Canada.

Printed and bound in the U.S.A.

Table of Contents

CHAPTER ONE

I'll Take That

The witch's gnarled and twisted hands grasped the stick firmly and stirred the contents of the cauldron. She was the eldest and also the most ugly of the three. Her huge hooked nose stopped just short of touching her top lip and when she spoke you could see that the few remaining teeth she had were blackened and broken with age. She had lost an eye years before in a battle with a winter witch, but rather than wear an eye patch, she simply left the empty socket exposed, black and gruesome.

She began to mumble as she continued stirring, "The freshly cut tail of a gerbil, the liver of a brand new puppy, the heart of a newborn lamb."

She cackled and looked at her two sisters. "So far, so good," she said as her mouth twisted into what was more of an ugly grimace than a smile. "Fetch me the spell book, one of you. Quickly, so that I can see what other ingredients we need."

The witch nearest her went to fetch the book, her huge black dress rustling as she did. Like the others, she was dressed entirely in black from the top of her pointed hat to the tip of her large feet which were clad in huge, black buckled shoes. As with most witches, she had an abundance of warts scattered all over her face, the largest of which hung from the tip of her nose. Unlike her other sisters, though, her eyes were not small and beady. They were a piercing silver and they glinted dangerously as she looked around for the misplaced spell book.

"Over there," said the third sister, pointing as she spoke. But it was not a finger she pointed with, for this sister also had fought a hard battle with the same winter witch years ago and lost, forfeiting her right hand and part of her arm in the process. Her hand and arm were now made of strong metal and though at first the witch had felt disadvantaged, she was now able to accomplish most tasks better than ever before.

She had been able to slit the young pup's tummy, for example, without even having to use a knife, and acquiring the gerbil's tail had been easy and quite enjoyable.

She watched as her sister's eyes shone silver in the darkness as she bent to lift the spell book and bring it back to the fire over which the cauldron bubbled. Just then, there was a huge clap of thunder as the sky grew even darker than before. Lightning forked across the sky and the three witches cackled together at the thought of the impending storm.

"A perfect night, sisters," said the first sister, her stagnant breath mixing with the night air as she spoke. She stopped turning the pages when she reached the spell they were looking for. She ran her blackened fingernail down the page until she found the next ingredient she must put into the cauldron.

"Aha!" She grinned maliciously. "This is one I'm going to enjoy. A young boy's freshly severed finger." She looked at her two sisters and they grinned back. "Bring him to me," she growled.

The two sisters looked delightedly at one another and left the orange glow of the flames, heading toward the bushes that encircled the clearing where they had built their fire. The boy whimpered as they approached. His wrists were raw and bleeding from his struggle to free himself from the thick ropes the witches had used to bind his arms and legs together. His blond hair hung limply on his forehead and tearstains marked his face. He had tried to be brave, after all, thirteen-year-old boys don't cry, but he simply couldn't help it. He was really afraid.

The one with the silver eyes was staring at him, her eyes seeming to burn right through him, as though seeing into his very soul. The other one bent down and released his feet from the ropes with one quick snip from her metal hand. He shivered involuntarily.

"Stand up, boy," she ordered, dragging him toward her as she spoke. The boy winced, partly from the pain of her grasp and also at the sharpness of the odor emanating from both witches.

If I live to be one hundred, he thought, I shall never forget that smell...that is if I live at all.

He was forced to walk toward the cauldron, while thunder clapped and bolts of lightning shot across the sky. As he drew closer to the fire, he could see that the eldest witch was bending down to unwrap something. She unraveled a large piece of black cloth, uncovering a vast selection of shiny steel knives.

The boy drew in his breath sharply. He started to shake almost uncontrollably.

The witch seemed unable to make up her mind about which knife would be best to use and was debating intently over two in particular.

When he was close enough, his two captors pushed him to his knees and began to untie his hands. The witch still looked at the knives.

"If I may make a suggestion, sister," began one, "if you're having difficulty choosing, I could sever the finger now."

She clicked her metal fingers in the air, and the boy began to cry openly.

"Shut up, sniveling little coward," said the witch, deciding eventually on a knife and lifting it into the air with a flourish. She had placed a large rock on the ground and now indicated to her sisters that they should position the boy's hand on top.

He was sobbing now and pleading with them.

"Please," he begged. "Please let me go! Please don't hurt me!"

Annoyed at the boy's struggles and pleas, the witch lifted the knife high into the air.

"Ready?" she asked her two sisters, who

restrained the boy on either side.

They both nodded. As the knife drew closer to his hand, the child screamed and tried in vain to pull away. The cold steel glinted as it made contact and his finger cleanly and neatly severed from his hand, fell noiselessly onto the grass. Blood spurted from the gaping wound, and the witches left the boy to fall down in agony as they watched their sister excitedly lift the severed finger and throw it into the cauldron. Another bolt of thunder followed and they clapped their hands in glee and danced hysterically around the fire.

Two young girls dressed in matching leotards and tap dance shoes walked in front of the steaming cauldron and held up a large sign. Just before the curtain fell, the audience was able to read the sign.

END OF ACT ONE.

CHAPTER TWO

The Wart

Their black costumes, hats, and shoes discarded now in favor of their school uniforms, the three girls sat together in the school cafeteria discussing the rehearsal.

"Don't know if these plastic warts were a good idea," moaned Melissa as she looked in her mirror. "This one on my chin's really stuck. Where on earth did you get them?" she asked Jo.

"From the joke shop in town," replied her friend. "The same place I got the severed finger—wasn't it great?"

"Not as great as these donuts," said Danny Cottrill as he swiped one of their donuts.

"Hey!" cried Jenny, jumping to her feet. "Give that back!"

Danny stopped and turned to face the girls. "Why? What happens if I don't?" He smirked. "Will you cast a spell on me?" And he stuffed half of the stolen donut into his mouth.

"Yeah," shouted Jenny. "You watch yourself, Danny Cottrill, or I'll get my spell book and turn you into a fat, ugly toad. Whoops," she giggled, "I almost forgot—you already are a fat, ugly toad." And she sat back down beside her two friends.

Danny had been too busy laughing at his own joke to hear the last part of what Jenny had to say and made his way through the busy cafeteria, slapping people (who didn't want to be slapped) hard on the back of the head, tripping smaller kids carrying trays of food, and stealing anything within reach.

"Bully," mumbled Melissa, returning her gaze to the mirror and making renewed efforts to remove the offending wart.

"Oh, I wish this thing would just come off," she groaned in exasperation, just as the piece of plastic loosened its grip from her chin and fell onto the table in front of her.

"There ya go!" Jo smiled. "And I didn't even see you cast a spell!"

Melissa smiled back at her friend. "Didn't you hear me utter the magic words: Hocus Pocus. You can wish for anything your heart desires you know, acne-free skin, a spot on the soccer team, a date with Jonathan..."

The three girls sighed as one.

"If only," Melissa sighed. "The day one of us manages to get a date with Jonathan will be nothing short of a miracle."

Jo rubbed at her fingernails. The black nail polish she had just removed had left little flecks on her cuticles.

"Great rehearsal though, girls. Don't you think?

I'm so glad Miss Dobson found the play. It's so dramatic. You could almost hear the sixth graders hold their breath this morning when we rehearsed act one."

Jenny agreed, "Yeah, but I have to admit it's a relief taking the fake arm off after rehearsal. It's hard to maneuver the fingers."

"We could change it, I guess," said Melissa. "I mean, it's not like a mechanical arm was in the original play. Miss Dobson just thought it made *Oh Spirits Obey Us* more updated."

"No, she's right," said Jenny, flexing her hand and fingers. "We should leave it in. It does make the play a little more modern. But wasn't Jonathan great this morning," she sighed longingly. "Those screams were really bloodcurdling, I almost believed him. Anyway, where did you say Miss Dobson got the script from?" She turned to Melissa.

"Apparently," said her friend, "she was cleaning out an old drawer in the drama room a few weeks ago when she came across it. She read it over and liked it instantly, and when she looked in old school records she realized that although it was actually written by a former student, it had never been performed. According to what she was told, all previous attempts to stage the play had ended in failure since the students playing the parts of the witches' enemies had to leave school due to mysterious illnesses. Weird, don't you think?"

"Definitely and just a teensy bit scary," agreed Jo.

"Oh, don't be silly," said Jenny. "You're getting carried away with all this talk of puppies' livers and lambs' hearts. It's just a story."

Just then, the bell rang, signaling the end of lunch. Jenny scrambled on the floor, grabbing the books that had fallen out of her bag and stuffing them back in.

"Gotta go!" she called over her shoulder, after quickly finishing her juice. "I have history next. See you at 3 o'clock."

Jo and Melissa waved goodbye to their friend and made their way to the opposite end of the school.

"Math—ugh!" groaned Melissa, as the two entered the classroom.

"Yeah," whispered Jo, "but at least the view is nice."

Both girls laid their chins on their hands and gazed dreamily at Jonathan for the rest of class.

CHAPTER THREE

The Crow

The next morning the three friends were back in drama, though this time they were not on stage. Instead, the girls were going through some of the scene changes with Miss Dobson.

"I hate this part," muttered Melissa under her breath. "It's just so boring."

"What was that, Melissa?" asked her teacher. "Please, share whatever little gem you just imparted with the rest of the class."

Melissa cleared her throat and stood up.

"I'm sorry, I was just saying to Jenny what a good idea it had been to have a dress rehearsal yesterday," she said nervously.

Miss Dobson raised an eyebrow, not believing a word the girl said.

"Okay, Melissa, sit down and let's continue. We only have a couple of weeks left, you know. First night will be upon us before we know it."

Eventually, after much discussion about lighting changes, who should exit when, and so on, Miss Dobson called the three girls to the front of the stage.

"Okay, girls, we're going to rehearse the scene in the mortuary where the witches bring a dead body back to life. Remember, do your best! I want gruesome! I want evil! Now terrify me."

Miss Dobson took her place with the rest of the class as the three witches began. She had to admit, as they quickly got into character, they were very good. They were incredibly realistic, and she actually wondered at one point if the play was going to be too scary for some of the younger students. She shook her head dismissively.

No, she concluded. Kids these days grow up so quickly. It would take a lot more than a play about witches to scare them. Everything would be just fine.

On stage, the three girls had joined hands and with their eyes tightly closed, they walked around the mortuary slab (or desk which would be adapted on the night of the play), slowly circling the stiff, cold body positioned there motionless and draped in a white sheet. They mumbled incantations as they walked, and Miss Dobson made a mental note to tell them to speak up a little as she was unsure which particular chant they were repeating.

She glanced sideways toward the drama room window and noticed how dark the sky had suddenly become.

There must be a big thunderstorm coming, she thought as she turned her attention back to the stage.

They really were very good, she thought again as she watched the girls in action. The atmosphere was electric, and you could have heard a pin drop in the room.

The witches had stopped circling the body and now took their places, one at either end of the body and one in the center. Placing their fingertips on different parts of the body, they began to hum quietly, gradually building up the noise until the room was filled with it. Then, as one, they stopped.

"He grows warm," said the first witch.

The witch at the center of the body smiled.

"Let us complete our task," replied the third witch.

Keeping one hand on the corpse and pressing the palms of the others together, they started to recite the words they hadn't said together for hundreds of years.

"From cold and dark, we bid you rise. More time on earth will be your prize. To spread more evil, cast black spells, come back to us from the place you now dwell."

They chanted the spell, over and over, their words coming faster, almost tripping over one another, until it was almost impossible to make out the words clearly.

The whole time, the sky was getting darker and darker. Miss Dobson watched, fascinated, as the "dead body" underneath the white sheet started to rise, as if it was responding to the witches' incantations.

Suddenly, the window at the far end of the room broke and shattered into a million tiny pieces.

One of the girls who watched the play and sat closest to the window jumped up in fright and began to cry. Startled, Miss Dobson got to her feet and quickly hit the light switch. The room was so dark you would have sworn it was closer to midnight than the middle of the afternoon.

"Okay, everyone, calm down," she shouted, as her students clamored to see what had happened to the window. "Stay back," she ordered. "I don't want any of you cutting yourselves on the glass."

As she bent down to take a closer look, she was able to see the reason for the broken window. A small crow, no more than a few weeks old, was sprawled in the middle of the shattered glass.

It must have left the nest too soon and smashed right into the window, she thought, shaking her head. I wouldn't have thought one little bird would have been enough to break the window though. I guess the glass must not be that strong and the slightest thing would have broken it.

She took her handkerchief from her pocket and gathered up the tiny bird.

"Stand back, girls. Come on now, everything's all right."

Melissa, Jo, and Jenny had come off the stage and joined the rest of the class looking curiously at the broken window. Miss Dobson placed the small dead bird in her trash can. She would ask the janitor to remove it later.

She then looked up at the desk on stage with the white sheet draped over it. She climbed up the few steps to the stage and stood facing her class.

"Well done, everyone, that was great! I'll see you tomorrow for an extra rehearsal."

As the bell rang, she raised her voice to try and be heard over it. "Trolls and hobgoblins, be ready tomorrow. And remember to bring your costumes if they're ready!"

As the class noisily gathered their things together and left the room, Miss Dobson glanced again at the white sheet. She could have sworn something had moved when the girls were reciting their lines, but that was just plain silly. She had simply been carried away with the atmosphere, the darkening sky, and the threat of thunder and lightning.

Anxiously, she edged toward the desk. Gingerly, and more afraid than she would have cared to admit, she lifted the edge and looked underneath. She exhaled loudly, realizing then that she had been holding her breath. A bunch of books and an old pair of shoes! She should have known better! She put the sheet back gently and smiled to herself, relieved.

It wasn't until she had closed the door of the drama room behind her that she realized just how loudly her heart was beating.

CHAPTER FOUR

When You Wish Upon a Witch

Jenny looked in dismay at the test paper in front of her. She hated math. No matter how hard she tried, she felt like she would never understand it, and it would always be unfamiliar to her, like a foreign language.

"Oh, I wish I could do this," she muttered, running her fingers through her hair and chewing on the end of her pencil. Reluctantly, she put pencil to paper and started to work her way through the test.

Two days later, when Mr. Carter handed out the test papers, he flashed Jenny a huge smile.

"Great work, Jenny," he congratulated her.

"You must have put in a lot of hours studying! I'm thrilled."

Jenny looked in disbelief at her paper. A+! She checked her name at the top of the page, thinking Mr. Carter had handed her the wrong one, but no, it was her.

Jo looked at her questioningly, and Jenny passed her the paper.

"Wow," whispered her friend. "How did you do that?"

Jenny shrugged and opened her textbook ready for that day's lesson.

Who cares how she did it, she had received an A+ in a subject she had never understood. Maybe it was starting to sink in, finally.

Weeks—even months—later when the girls looked back at the events surrounding the play, they would realize just how early their wishes had begun to come true. Silly things like Melissa wishing her wart would come off, Jenny's math test, and later, Jo wishing her mom would buy her new shoes.

No sooner had they voiced their wishes, they happened. But they didn't start to get spooked until the day they wished harm on Danny Cottrill.

The sun was shining and most of the students were outside for Sports Day. The events were taking place in different parts of the field, but the girls were watching the hurdles as Jonathan, their crush, was the favorite to win.

The starting gun was fired, and the boys started running. Jonathan was on the outside of the track and on his right was Danny Cottrill. The boys were almost neck and neck for most of the race until Danny fell and as he did, he seemed to deliberately stick his foot out in front of Jonathan, causing him to tumble to the ground.

"Jerk!" shouted Melissa. "Why'd he have do that? Jonathan was going to win for sure if Danny hadn't pulled him down with him!" She sat down, disgusted by what she had seen.

Jenny agreed, "Sometimes I really wish he would get hurt so he knows what it feels like. He's such a bully!"

The race continued, of course, and Jonathan slowly got to his feet, checking for injuries as he did. He had cut his knee and limped over to Danny to offer him a helping hand. But Danny wasn't moving.

Jonathan leaned closer, just as the school nurse ran on to the track.

"He must have knocked himself out when he fell," said Jonathan. "Maybe he has a concussion."

The nurse quickly checked the boy and decided that the best course of action was to call for an ambulance.

Danny was carried off the track and with the lights flashing and siren wailing, he was taken to the hospital.

The next morning, the principal, Mr. Perrie, called an assembly to inform the school of Danny's injuries. Not only had the boy broken both of his legs when he fell, he had also slipped into a coma. His family was with him and had been told that things were scary for Danny, but they could hope for recovery.

Jenny covered her mouth with her hands.

"Oh..." she breathed deep, as Melissa and Jo looked at her. "I wished that on him. Remember? I actually wished Danny would get hurt."

"Oh, don't be silly, Jenny," began Jo. "You can't wish someone into a coma!"

"You can't?" asked Jenny. "I'm not so sure. Let's take a long, hard look at what's been happening over the past few weeks."

The girls had by now left the assembly hall and had stopped outside their next class.

Aided by Jenny, Melissa started recounting all the things they had wished for that had come true.

Although skeptical to begin with, there were so many things that had actually come true that Jo had to agree there was more than sheer coincidence involved.

"But how? I mean, I don't understand why all of a sudden this would be happening to us," said Jo. "How many times have you closed your eyes and made a wish, hoping it would come true? But of course, it never does. So now, for some inexplicable reason, we're being granted everything we ask for. Why?"

"The play," said Jenny, quietly. "I think everything is somehow linked to the play. Think about it, this all started to happen when we took on the roles of the witches."

Mrs. Cadzow leaned on the doorjamb and looked over at the three girls.

"Is there something I should know, girls? Have you been excused from my class and no one bothered to tell me?" she asked.

"Oh, sorry," stuttered Melissa, as the three girls made their way into the classroom.

Before Melissa took her seat, she whispered to her two friends, "Remember that old saying, 'Be very careful what you wish for. It just might come true.' I think we should start being careful about..."

"MELISSA!" shouted Mrs. Cadzow. "Are you or are you not a member of this class? If you are, please sit down, take out your books, and pay attention to today's lesson."

The bell signaling the end of their day seemed to take forever to ring. The girls gathered at the school gates, and Melissa took her copy of the play from her bag.

"Geraldine Somers," she read aloud. "She was the person who wrote the play. I think we should start doing a bit of research on her. The more time I've had to think about these wishes, the more convinced I am it has something to do with the play, and the author seems as good a person to start with as any."

Jenny and Jo nodded in agreement.

"Let's see, tomorrow is Saturday, so we can go to the library in the morning and see if we can find any record of her," said Melissa. "Maybe we can find out where she lives now, if she's written any other plays, and so on."

"But remember," said Jo, "wasn't this play written at least sixty years ago? If Geraldine was, say, thirteen or fourteen when she wrote it, she's probably pretty old by now. We'll have to be careful if we do find her. We don't want to go upsetting an old lady."

Agreeing to meet the following morning at 9 a.m. sharp outside the library, the girls parted ways.

CHAPTER FIVE

Reluctant Research

The girls had been searching unsuccessfully for the better part of an hour when suddenly Melissa found what she was looking for.

"There she is," she said excitedly, running her finger down the page. "Look! Geraldine Somers, born October 7, 1940. That means she must be in her eighties by now. So if she wrote the play when she was about our age, it's actually over sixty-five years old. Now, where does she live?"

"Look, Melissa," said Jo quietly, pointing to the opposite side of the page. Under the farthest column, an entry had been written in showing that Geraldine Somers had died on April 14, 1982.

Jo sighed. "That's that then. We can't exactly talk to a ghost," she said.

The three girls stood silently staring at the information on the page. What could they do now besides forget the whole thing?

Jenny closed the book and put it back on the shelf they had taken it from. "Come on, you two, let's go. No point in standing here."

Jenny linked arms with her two friends and the three left the library.

Suddenly, Melissa stopped.

"Wait a minute," Melissa said to her two friends. "We can visit the grave, right? She must be buried in the local cemetery. Her last known address in the book was in town, so it makes sense that she would be buried here. Yes, that's it." She nodded her head excitedly. "We'll go visit her grave."

Jenny and Jo looked at each other, both feeling a lot less enthusiastic than Melissa seemed to be.

"Melissa, I don't see the point of..." began Jo.

"The point is," interrupted Melissa, "that it's the only starting point we have. Don't you see? We have nowhere else to go. We have to visit the grave. We simply have to if we want to find out anything. Jenny?" She looked at her other friend.

"Well," began Jenny, slowly, "I guess I would like to get to the bottom of what's been going on, but I don't know if..."

"It's settled then," Melissa interrupted again. "Let's go, it won't take us long to walk there."

"Melissa, wait," said Jenny. "I can't go right now. I have to go shopping with my mom this afternoon, and if we walk to and from the cemetery, I won't be back in time to meet her. I'm either going to have to opt out or do this later."

Melissa looked at Jo.

"Sorry, Melissa, I promised to take my niece ice-skating this afternoon. I could go with you when I get back though. I should be home around four."

Melissa sighed heavily, disappointed that they

couldn't begin right away. She wasn't exactly known for her patience.

"Okay," she agreed reluctantly. "Can we all meet at the gates of the graveyard at 4:30 p.m.? That should give us just enough daylight hours to find the gravestone and check things out. And remember, wear something warm, it'll be really cold up there."

The local cemetery was located at the very top of a steep hill and was notoriously cold, especially on a dark November night.

Jo trembled inwardly at the thought of what they were going to be doing later that evening, but said nothing, not wanting to put a damper on Melissa's plans.

As they went their separate ways, Melissa shouted over her shoulder to one of the girls to remember to bring a flashlight and a stake—just in case.

"In case of what?" Jo glanced worriedly at Jenny.

"Vampires," Jenny told her friend. Then, seeing the look of horror on her friend's face, she laughed.

"It's a joke."

"Honestly, she's joking," said Melissa. "There's no such thing, Jo. You've been watching too many scary movies."

Jo grinned sheepishly. "No, no, I knew the whole time she was joking. Really, I did!"

Jenny slipped her arm through Jo's.

"It's all right, Jo. I'm not too happy about going to a graveyard either, but it'll be fine. You'll see."

CHAPTER SIX

REALLY Reluctant Research

Melissa looked at her watch. Four thirty on the dot. Where were they? Just then, she heard the chatter of their voices as they reached the top of the hill and joined her.

"...and that was when I had to have the bandage applied," finished Jo. "So embarrassing! There was Katy, skating and twirling like a professional, and I had to go and fall. And of course it just wouldn't stop bleeding, which was awful, but when the attendant insisted I go and visit the treatment room, I thought I would die of shame. I mean, I'm going to have a scar on my knee which will be just perfect for the Christmas dance."

"Hey, Melissa! Been here long?" asked Jenny.

Melissa shifted, stamping her feet in an attempt to keep warm. "No," she replied with a half smile. "I just got here."

It really was bitterly cold that night. The paths leading throughout the cemetery glistened with frost in the semi-darkness.

"Okay," said Melissa, taking charge as always, "here is the plan. I think we have to split up, each of us taking a section of the graveyard until we find the grave. There's just no point in us covering the same ground together. So what do you think of us going on our own now and meeting back here in two hours? That should give us enough time."

"But what if we find the grave before that?" asked Jenny.

"Well, the cemetery isn't that big," said Melissa, thoughtfully. "What about if we make our way to the mausoleum in an hour and a half? Do you think that would be enough time?"

Jenny shivered involuntarily at the use of the word "mausoleum."

The grand, imposing building that stood at the edge of the cemetery had been erected hundreds of years ago by a Mr. Carruthers in memory of his wife. It stood, a proud monument to the memory of Mrs. Carruthers, and now housed not only her body, but also that of Mr. Carruthers and most of the Carruthers family.

Though Jenny would admit that it was a beautiful building, it gave her the creeps. She tended to hurry past it as quickly as she could if she ever had to go that way.

She glanced at the building's tall domes then looked away quickly. What she really wanted to do right now was turn on her heels and go back home. She hated scary things and places, and she especially hated how she was so easily coerced into doing things she didn't want to. She sighed. She really liked Melissa and Jo and didn't want to let them down.

"Sure," she said, with mock enthusiasm. "That should be fine. Who's taking which path?"

After some discussion, the girls set off, each with their own private thoughts, and each equally determined to be the one to find the gravestone first. The graveyard forked off into three different roads and the girls took one each.

Jenny was more determined than the others, mostly so that she would be back home before darkness really started to fall. She wanted this search to be over with as quickly as possible.

Jenny walked along slowly, scanning each stone as she walked.

David Fisher
Beloved husband and father.
1902-1964

Suzanna Bellingham

Our beautiful daughter, gone to be with the angels.

1935-1942

Jenny stopped and stared. How awful, she thought, losing your child when she was so young. She wondered what had happened to the little girl, an accident maybe or an illness which could probably be cured nowadays but maybe not back in 1942. She tore herself away and tried to concentrate.

"Come on, Jen," she chastised herself. "You're not here to ponder over people's deaths. You're here to find Geraldine's grave."

She moved on, her eyes concentrating on the name on each gravestone.

She did come across a Geraldine once, but the last name was wrong and the dates didn't fit.

She walked past gravestones that were so old they had toppled over. She passed others that had fresh flowers strewn in front of them. She couldn't quite make up her mind which ones she disliked most.

After an hour, she had covered one whole side of the path and turned to make her way back down the other side.

It was getting darker now, and she found that she was having to step closer to the graves to make out the inscriptions. She was sorry she had forgotten to bring a flashlight and wondered how the other two girls were doing.

Halfway back down the path, she felt the first splash of rain.

Great, she thought, just what you want. Stuck in the middle of a graveyard on a cold November night with rain pouring down on top of you!

She squinted up at the blackening sky. The rain grew heavier and she quickened her pace, making her way toward the mausoleum. If she was lucky, either Jo or Melissa would have found the grave by now and they could all get out of this place.

The remaining gravestones were merely given

quick glances as Jenny walked now in the direction of the mausoleum.

There was no sign of her two friends when she walked up. Jenny stood outside for a few minutes, the rain much heavier now, dripping off her jacket and soaking into her jeans.

They must have gone inside, she thought. You'd have to be nuts to stand out here getting wet.

She turned and walked up the few steps to the mausoleum door and turned the handle. The solid door opened slowly, just wide enough for her to see inside. She caught her breath. It was as dark inside as it was outside in the cemetery and everything smelled damp and musty. She stepped forward. To her right, she could see the tomb erected by Mr. Carruthers in memory of his wife. The white marble tomb was just visible in the darkness, as were the stone pillars placed at each corner. Ornate drawings and inscriptions adorned the walls, though Jenny could not make out exactly what they were.

"Melissa? Jo?" she tried to call, though her voice was no more than a whisper. She cleared her throat and tried again, calling to her friends louder this time.

She had started to edge her way forward now and was aware of another huge tomb on her left. This one had the body shape of a man carved in marble etched on top of it. Jenny, her eyes growing more accustomed to the darkness, could make out the outline of his face.

How creepy, she thought, unable to understand why anyone would want a likeness of themselves put in such an awful place—a place that smelled like rotting flesh and death.

She heard scuffling at her feet and jumped, her hand brushing one of the tombs as she did. Though she couldn't be sure, she thought she saw a tail disappear through a hole in the wall.

Oh no, rats, she thought. She immediately considered running back outside. She steadied herself and removed her hand from the tomb. It felt wet and slimy. She lifted it closer to her face and saw that her hand was coated in slime, and parts of it appeared to be moving.

Maggots! They were crawling all over the tomb and all over her! She tried to shake the horrible creatures from her hand and barely managed to stifle a scream as she turned to run. She could see that thousands of maggots were pouring from the eyes and nose of the marble figure on the tomb.

She knew she had to get out of there fast. But at that exact moment, the heavy wooden door banged shut behind her.

CHAPTER SEVEN

Three Witches

"Jenny! Over here!" she heard her friend's voice say. "We've been waiting for you."

She looked down toward the front of the mausoleum and was able to make out the figures of Melissa and Jo.

Thank God, she thought, stifling a small sob as she began walking toward her two friends.

"I'm so happy to see you," shouted Jenny. "I just had the most awful experience. I really think we should get out of here now."

Melissa and Jo half turned toward her.

"Don't be silly," said Melissa. "Everything's all right now. Come on, come and sit beside me."

The two girls were sitting on a low bench in front of a raised up platform, almost like an altar. As Melissa turned fully toward her friend, she stretched out both arms to her. Except that something was missing.

"Your hand!" gasped Jenny, stepping back in horror. "What happened to your hand?"

Melissa's hand was no longer there, instead her arm seemed to stop just inside the sleeve of her jacket.

"I don't understand," gasped Jenny. "Are you messing with me?" she sobbed. "Because if you are, it's definitely not funny."

She turned to her other friend. "Jo, talk to me."

"Calm down," began Jo. "There's no need to get hysterical."

As Jenny turned to look at her friend, she gasped in horror and screamed. Jo's right eye was missing.

"Don't scream, silly girl," said Jo. "It's only an eye socket. I didn't know you could be such a baby."

Jenny covered her face with both her hands. She must be having a bad dream. There was no other explanation for this. She opened her eyes and looked again at her two friends.

To her horror, Melissa and Jo were now undergoing some sort of bizarre transformation before her very eyes. Their skin had turned brown and cracked before it started to fall in small pieces from their faces. Underneath were much older faces that Jenny recognized as belonging to the witches from the play. Their faces were covered in warts, lined and wrinkled. They had huge, hooked noses and blackened stumpy teeth. Their clothes fell away and were replaced by the black cloaks Jenny had by now become familiar with. A foul odor then permeated the mausoleum. Jenny was now completely terrified.

She wanted to run, but knew she had to pass the tombs containing the rotting dead bodies and the floor that seemed to be squirming with maggots.

She felt herself being prodded from behind and turned around to see who was there. She drew in a breath sharply. It was the third witch. The one whose part she took in the play.

"What are you doing? What do you want from me?" Jenny asked falteringly.

"We don't want anything from you, my dear," replied one of the witches. "It's what you want from us that matters, don't you see?"

"N-no, I'm afraid I don't," said Jenny as she tried to stop her voice from wavering.

The three witches now encircled her. Their fetid breaths touched her face as they walked slowly around with their dusty black cloaks billowing around their feet.

"So naïve, so unutterably naïve," cackled the witch who was missing an eye. "The play, my pretty one, the play! *Oh Spirits Obey Us*, remember? The one you're performing at school? Don't you know what it's about? Don't you know how dangerous it

is to dabble in witchcraft when you know nothing about it?"

"B-but, it's only a play," stammered Jenny, desperately trying to keep calm.

The witches stopped moving.

"Only a play, is it?" said the first witch in a menacingly low voice. "You silly girl, don't you know anything? You can't just recite spells, dabble in witchcraft, and chop off fingers, then just walk away from it. It's a very dangerous thing, you know."

She pushed her face closer to Jenny's, and the young girl recoiled as far as she could, only to be pushed forward again by the bony fingers of the witch behind her.

"We didn't really ch-chop the finger off," she stuttered. "We only pretended to."

"Shut up," the witch snarled. "I'm the one who's speaking."

She ran her bony fingers through Jenny's hair, causing the frightened girl to shiver but still stand her ground nonetheless.

"Aha, she has guts, has she?" cackled the witch as the girl stood firm. "Why do you think we waited for you this evening? We wanted to offer you something, my pretty."

The witch looked at her sisters and both nodded and smirked in the girl's direction.

Using the one hand she did possess, she took hold of Jenny's. Her fingers were long, bony, and unbelievably cold. Jenny desperately wanted to pull away.

"How would you like to join us?" she asked the girl. "Become a witch—a real witch—not someone playing a part in a play. Someone who can do this!" And she spat at the girl's feet.

Jenny looked down and saw the witch's spittle spread and grow bigger on the floor of the mausoleum until it gradually began to take shape.

First, the tail developed, followed by the long, sharp teeth and furry body, until the spit had turned into a large brown rat! The biggest rat that Jenny had ever seen.

Jenny moved her feet backwards, but noted that the rat did not move away, seeming content to stare at her from its position on the floor.

The witch smiled a broad, almost toothless, smile, and her two sisters cackled with laughter.

The one with the missing eye clapped her hands and said, "Well done, sister! I'd forgotten that old trick."

She too spat on the floor, her spittle also spreading and becoming larger before transforming into another rat. This one even bigger than the first. Not to be outdone, the third sister repeated the process, and soon there were dozens of rats, some brown, some black, but none of them moving and all of them seeming to stare right at Jenny.

"Please, let me wake up," the young girl prayed. "Let me open my eyes so this nightmare can be over."

She closed her eyes and blinked hard, but when

she opened them again, the scene in front of her was exactly as it had been before.

"We're still here, my dear," cackled the first witch, almost as though she were able to read the young girl's mind. "And we're still looking for recruits. Come on, my pretty." She rubbed her bony finger along the girl's chin. "You'd have such fun, you know. Let's see, now, who else do you dislike, besides young Danny Cottrill?"

The witch smiled and continued, "We sorted him out for you. He's still on life support, but you could be the one to perform the magic, Jenny. You! You could cast the evil spells. You need not be afraid of anyone again. No one would ever be able to hurt you. We could give you that power. Come on now, what do you say?"

Jenny was horrified. "Danny? You did that to Danny? How could you, how awful..."

The witch interrupted, "No, my dear, you did it. You wished harm on the boy, did you not? And since we have to obey you, in accordance with the title of the play, we were only carrying out your wishes."

"But everyone says things they don't mean sometimes," said Jenny. "I didn't really want anything bad to happen to Danny." She moved her foot slightly, looking down as she did so. The rats still stared up at her but none of them moved.

"Then you'll have to be more careful about what you wish for, won't you? But I'm not at all convinced that I believe you. I think you'd make a great witch, and we're so in need of some young blood."

She moved toward the girl, kicking one of the rats as she did so. The rat reacted for the first time, angrily biting at Jenny's ankle as though she were to blame. Jenny cried out and bent to rub her ankle.

"Please let me go," she pleaded with the witches. "Please, my parents will be wondering where I am. I have to go home, please."

"Don't be silly, we can't let you go now. You're going to be one of us. Be patient, dear, we just have to recite a little spell. It won't take long. Come, sisters, join hands and you, my dear, you must concentrate on what we are saying, for you will have to join with us at the end and take a vow to be a follower of all things evil."

The witches started their chant, walking slowly around the girl. The rats scuttled in all directions in order to escape the sharp kick of the witches' feet.

Jenny was trembling from head to toe and tried desperately to think of a way out. If she could just break though the witches' hands and run toward the entrance to the mausoleum, she would maybe avoid the rats. However, she would be sure to run into the millions of slimy maggots that were crawling all over the tombs and the floor. She swallowed hard. She decided she could stand the maggots. She just had to get out of there.

As she looked up toward the back of the mausoleum, she saw to her horror that one of the tombs was opening. A skeletal hand was pushing

back the marble lid and she could just see the skull-
like head beginning to appear.

Jenny fainted.

CHAPTER EIGHT

The Voice

Meanwhile, outside in the cemetery, Melissa and Jo—the real Melissa and Jo—had found the grave of Geraldine Somers. They had bumped into one another just outside the mausoleum, both having exhausted the graves in the parts of the cemetery they had explored. It was then that by chance they spotted a few graves tucked away in the corner just beside the entrance. Sure enough, there it was, clearly engraved with the author's name. Both girls bent down, wiping the rain out of their eyes.

"Geraldine Somers. We found you at last," said Melissa.

She brushed her fingers over the lettering on the

grave, taking in the woman's date of birth and when she died, and thinking how plain and unobtrusive the lettering was in comparison to some of the stones she had seen earlier. There was a vase of fairly fresh flowers placed at the foot of the grave, and Melissa wondered who had placed them there.

"So you found me, girls," said a soft voice.

Jo and Melissa looked quizzically at one another.

"Who said that? Jenny?" Jo asked.

The girls looked around.

The howling of the wind and the steady beat of the rain as it splashed heavily onto the ground sounded in their ears. Melissa pushed her hair back from her face and smiled at Jo.

"We're hearing things. The wind is just playing tricks on us, that's all," she said.

But again they heard the voice, still soft but a little clearer.

"I've been waiting for you, girls. I'm so glad you're here at last."

The two girls stood up, almost falling backward in their haste.

"Where is it coming from?" asked Jo as she grabbed Melissa's arm. "I can hear a voice, but I can't see anyone."

"Please don't be afraid, girls." The voice was stronger and more insistent now. "I really must speak with you. Please, come closer to the stone. I need you both to listen to me very carefully."

Melissa and Jo looked at each other in bewilderment, but because they didn't know what else to do, they did as they were told and walked forward to kneel in front of the gravestone. As they knelt on the wet grass, there was an audible sigh of relief.

"Thank you, girls. I had hoped you'd be the ones to help, so please, listen very carefully to what I have to say. I am the spirit of Geraldine Somers. I no longer have the power to materialize. My spirit has been growing weaker over the years, and I am afraid that you will be unable to see me. You can, however, hear my voice and hopefully, once I have told you my story, you will be able to help."

The rain was beating down onto their bent forms, and the sky was almost completely black. Melissa and Jo were afraid. They no longer wanted to be there in the graveyard. They wanted to forget the whole idea of finding the author's grave and forget the entire play for that matter. But before either of the girls could move, the voice spoke again.

"The play, *Oh Spirits Obey Us*, you must know that I was the person responsible for writing it. God help me. I know that you two and your friend are playing the parts of the three witches and that is why I must speak to you. You see, although the play was written decades ago, it has never been performed on stage. There is always a series of accidents that befalls anyone who tries to help me stop the evil witches from carrying out their plan.

"Anyone who has played the parts of the witches

up until now has been very happy to have all their wishes come true and has been disinterested in helping me break the real witches' evil hold. So when I knew you girls weren't happy with recent events, well, it was like a breath of fresh air."

The voice paused briefly.

"It's all my fault," she began again. "I wrote the words to the play and unwittingly or not, I conjured up those evil sisters. Because of this I will have to be the one to cast them back into the darkness where they belong. Of course, I can't do it myself and so I have to put myself at your mercy and ask—no, plead—for you to help."

"But what can we do?" asked Melissa. "The witches can't be real, surely?"

She looked at Jo. Jo didn't reply but the look on her face said more than words ever could.

"Yeah, I know." Melissa nodded wryly. "I'm talking to a gravestone. How real can things get?"

The voice started again, "We don't have a lot

of time, girls. Please hear what I have to say. In the past, the girls playing the parts of the witches have seemed to actually take on their characters as well as the parts they are playing. Decent, well-mannered girls have turned into nasty, evil people who become accustomed to having their wishes come true. In the course of the rehearsals, anyone who is seen to oppose these girls has a tragic accident. Look back at the school records—you'll see that I'm telling the truth.

"If, however, the play ever does have an opening night, it must not be performed the way it was written. If it is, everyone who is in the audience will become spellbound.

"What you must try to do is change some parts of the play. It will break the spell and send the evil witches back to the depths. By doing so, you will also manage to free my trapped spirit. I can have no rest while the three witches are allowed to carry on their evil work."

Melissa wiped some rain from her face and sat back on her heels.

"I know this is quite a bit of information for you young girls to take in. And I know how unbelievable this whole story must seem to you, but I'm begging you both. Will you help?"

Before the girls could reply, they heard a loud scream coming from the direction of the mausoleum. Simultaneously, they jumped quickly to their feet and shouted, "Jenny!"

CHAPTER NINE

Please, Not Maggots

They both ran in the direction of the huge building and quickly climbed the stairs. As they pushed open the door, they were horrified by what they saw. Their eyes already accustomed to the darkness, they could clearly see their friend at the far end of the mausoleum. And she was not alone. Just as Geraldine Somers had said, the three witches were indeed walking the earth and practicing their evil magic. In fact, they were right here, surrounding their poor friend!

Melissa grabbed hold of Jo's hand.

"Come on, quickly! We have to help her."

Jo held back and said, "Melissa, look."

Melissa followed her friend's gaze to the moving carpet of maggots that lay before her. She gasped and put her hand to her mouth.

Not maggots, please, not maggots, she thought. She hated maggots.

They were everywhere, crawling over the tombs and even making their way up the pillars.

Swallowing hard, Melissa grabbed Jo's hand again.

"We have to do this," she said. "Come on, Jo. We have to help Jenny."

She would never forget the crunching noise under her feet as she and her friend went bravely forward into the heart of the mausoleum.

The witches were walking around Jenny in a circle now, and the two girls tried to conceal themselves behind one of the many pillars before deciding on the best way to get Jenny out of there.

When Melissa heard the scuttling noise at her feet, she didn't even have to look down to know it

was a rat running across the floor.

Jo stifled a scream and clung tightly to Melissa.

The witches' chant was growing louder, and the girls knew they would have to make a move soon if they were going to help Jenny.

At almost the same time as Jenny saw the tomb open, so did Melissa and Jo. But where Jenny mercifully fainted, there was no such release for the other two girls. They clung to each other in terror as the glowing red eyes of the skull emerged from the tomb.

"What's going on in there?" shouted a voice from the back of the mausoleum.

As the girls looked up, both doors were thrown open and two burly policemen, brandishing flashlights, came inside.

In an instant, the tomb lid slid back into place, the maggots disappeared, as did the rats, and the witches simply seemed to vanish into thin air.

Melissa and Jo ran from their hiding place to

the front of the mausoleum and knelt beside their friend.

Jo shook her shoulder.

"Jenny, Jenny, can you hear me? It's Jo. Jo and Melissa. Are you all right?"

Jenny's eyes opened slowly.

"Are they gone?" she asked, her voice no more than a whisper.

"They're gone, Jenny," Jo reassured her. "Everything's going to be all right. Can you sit up?"

Helped by Melissa and Jo, Jenny managed to pull herself into an upright position.

A brief flicker of fear crossed Jenny's face as she asked, "Are you really Jo and Melissa? You're not going to change into those awful spirits again, are you?"

Melissa held out both arms to hug her friend.

"It's really us, Jen," she said.

Jenny leaned forward into her friend's warm embrace.

"You've got both of your hands, Melissa." She smiled. "It really is you."

Just before she fainted for the second time that night, the two police officers heard her say, "And you have your eye back, Jo. I'm so glad you have your eye back."

"Concussion," one of the officers mouthed to the other. "Let's get her out of here."

CHAPTER TEN

A Plan

"You're very lucky, young lady," said the nurse at the hospital as she tucked Jenny's jeans back into her boots.

"I don't know whether it was a rat or not, but whatever nipped your ankle was prevented from breaking the skin by your boots."

"I-I'm not sure either," said Jenny.

The busy emergency room was so far removed from the horrors of the mausoleum that she began to wonder if she had imagined the whole thing. But then the nurse did say there was a mark on her ankle as if something had tried to bite her...

The nurse drew back the curtain and Melissa and

Jo were finally allowed to see their friend.

"Your mother should be here soon," said the nurse as she left to attend to the next patient. Then, putting her head back around the curtain, she said to the two girls, "Don't sit on the bed!"

Melissa and Jo got up from where they had positioned themselves on either side of their friend.

"Oops. All we seem to have done tonight is gotten ourselves into trouble." Melissa smiled.

"Yeah," agreed Jo. "Although I think I'd rather get into trouble with a nurse than three evil witches in a spooky graveyard."

"So, what now?" asked Jenny.

"Well, what you don't know is that while you were alone in the mausoleum, Jo and I found the grave of Geraldine Somers and spoke with her," said Melissa.

"Spoke with her? How can you talk to a ghost?" questioned Jenny, wondering if maybe she was suffering from a concussion.

Jo and Melissa exchanged amused glances.

"Yeah, we know it sounds bizarre," said Jo, "but it actually happened."

The two girls recounted word for word what Geraldine Somers had said to them from her grave. When they had finished, Jenny nodded her head slowly.

"It all makes sense, I guess. I didn't dream any of it, did I? The witches, the play, the missing hand and eye, the whole thing actually did happen. Gosh! What have we gotten ourselves mixed up in?"

"Tell me about it," said Melissa. "The question we have to ask ourselves now is do we believe Geraldine about all the problems surrounding the play and help her?"

"And everyone else," added Jo. "Remember what she said, if the play takes place on opening night and is performed word for word, everyone in the audience will be spellbound." She shook her head and looked down at the floor. "If you ask me," she said to her two friends, "we don't have a choice."

"But there are only a few days until opening night," said Jenny, "and a full dress rehearsal on Thursday. We don't have long to decide how we're going to sabotage the play."

Melissa looked thoughtful. "Geraldine said we couldn't follow the play word for word. So what if we change the words around? What if we don't recite the spells exactly as they're written, don't recite the chants like we're supposed to? That would work, right?" Melissa said, looking questioningly at her friends.

Jenny agreed. "Yes, that sounds like it could work, Melissa. But as soon as we get the words wrong someone else on stage or maybe even Miss Dobson will stop the play and correct us. How do we get around that problem?"

Melissa thought some more.

"We'll just miss rehearsals," she said slowly. "Don't you see? Miss Dobson would correct us in rehearsals, but there's no way she would stop and correct the real thing on opening night. Not with the audience full of parents and other teachers. It would be way too embarrassing to admit that your three leading ladies got it wrong!"

"And just how do we excuse ourselves from rehearsals?" asked Jo.

"Well, Jenny's got the perfect excuse. She hit her head and hurt her ankle, so she needs a few days to rest. No problem. And you and me? Hmm, let's see, a bad cold? A sore throat? Any sort of minor ailment would work," said Melissa. "Take your pick."

"And then we all make remarkable recoveries on opening night," said Jo. "By that time we've re-written the parts of the play we need to and learned all the new words!"

"Exactly!" Melissa smiled. "Leave the re-writes to me. I'll bribe my brother to bring them over to your houses, because if we're pretending to have colds and sore throats, I know for sure my parents won't let me leave the house. I knew my brother would come in handy someday!"

"The cemetery?" they heard a voice from the other end of the hallway say.

"Oh no, my mother," groaned Jenny, instantly feeling worse than she had before.

"Inside the mausoleum? What on earth was she doing in there? Where is she? Let me see her, please. Jenny? Jenny? Where are you?"

Her mother's high-pitched voice carried down the hospital hallway until her head poked around the curtain and she found her daughter. She threw her arms around the girl and hugged her so tightly that Jenny could hardly breathe.

"We'll head out," said Jo as she and Melissa started to leave.

Jenny tried to wave to her friends but her mother gripped her so tightly that she was unable to move her arms.

"Mom, I'm fine," she struggled to say. "Really, I

just fell, but nothing's broken."

"Fine? Fine?" screeched her mother. "Do you have any idea the things that have been running through my mind ever since the police knocked on my door this evening? And then to be told they found you in the mausoleum? What were you doing in there? You, Jenny, of all people! My Jenny, who's scared of her own shadow?"

"It's a long story, Mom, but right now I'm tired. Can I tell you later?"

"Tired?" questioned her mother. "But you can't sleep now, dear. You may have some sort of concussion. Did you hit your head when you fell? Wait there. Do you hear me? Don't move! I'm going to find a doctor to see exactly what condition you're in. Maybe you shouldn't come home with me tonight. Maybe you should spend a night here under observation."

As her mother left in search of a doctor, Jenny put her head back on her pillow and closed her eyes.

Her mother could be a lot to handle, but after her ordeal earlier that night, she actually found the high-pitched screech of her voice strangely reassuring. Maybe it was a concussion, after all…

CHAPTER ELEVEN

Rewrites

"Jo, where are you?" shouted Jo's dad from the hall downstairs.

"In the bathroom," the girl croaked. "What's wrong?"

"Melissa's younger brother just delivered a package for you. I'm headed to work, but I'll leave it on the counter. I'd bring it up, but I'm running late."

Jo appeared at the top of the stairway. "It's all right, Dad. I'll come down in a minute. Melissa said she'd send over some magazines for me. It's nothing important."

"Okay, gotta go! See you later sweetheart," her dad called as he wrestled with the door chain.

"Maybe if you put your briefcase down first?" suggested his daughter.

Putting down his briefcase with one hand and putting the half-eaten toast from the other hand into his mouth, her dad was able to release the security chain and open the front door.

"Bye," he called again and pulled the door shut behind him.

Jo shook her head. Fathers, she thought, they are worse than kids sometimes.

She bounded down the stairs and grabbed the brown envelope from its place on the counter. It had been a few days since the graveyard incident, and there was only one more day to go before the opening night of the play.

Jo made herself some toast and took the package and toast back upstairs to her bedroom. She opened her curtains a little to allow some gray November light into the room and settled down to look at Melissa's corrections.

At Jenny's house, Jenny scanned through the pages to see the changes Melissa had made. Her friend had used a yellow highlighter so that the alterations were easy to spot.

Jenny began learning her new lines. Whatever she did, she couldn't say the correct words on opening night. She had to concentrate and learn the spells the way Melissa had written them.

Meanwhile, in school, Miss Dobson was tearing her hair out.

"No, no, no," she admonished. "That's not when you're supposed to exit! You have to wait until the trolls enter, then you can leave."

She pushed her fingers through her already unruly hair and took a deep breath. She should have listened to the principal. He had told her about the play's history, and she had been stubborn enough to insist that she would be able to successfully stage a performance. Now look what had happened—her three leading girls were ill! All three of them! And on top of that, no one on stage seemed to have any idea where they were supposed to stand, not to mention what they were supposed to say. She wondered if they were aware what production they were starring in!

"Look, everyone, I know this is difficult," she began in the loudest voice she could muster. "Especially because we're missing our three witches, but their respective parents have assured me that they will be here on opening night. So for now, if we can just pretend they are here, use our imagination a little, and concentrate on the parts we're supposed to be playing, maybe we can get through this without me murdering one of you."

Some of the students giggled, forcing Miss Dobson to smile.

"And maybe we can actually make it to opening night and put on a performance both the school and your parents will be proud of."

There was lots of throat clearing and head nodding from the stage.

"Okay, from the beginning of that scene, Grant, please. And remember, hobgoblins do not chew bubblegum!"

CHAPTER TWELVE

This One's for You, Geraldine

A bouquet of flowers rested in the small sink in the principal's office. He would present them to Miss Dobson after the play that night.

He looked in the mirror to see that his tie was straight and wiped a chocolate crumb from the side of his mouth. That was the problem with these school performances, he found it so hard to resist the donations of home baking the mothers brought into the school. Especially Mrs. Castle's chocolate chip cookies. He moved the notch of his belt so it would sit easier on his ever-expanding waistline and left his office to make his way to the auditorium.

There was an air of excitement as people entered

the large room. Everyone attending would have someone close to them who would be performing on the stage that night, whether it be family or just the child of a friendly neighbor.

Younger brothers and sisters squirmed in their seats, most of them being kept quiet with a bar of chocolate in one hand and a soda in the other and the promise of ice cream after the show.

The stage itself had been designed by the cast, helped by Miss Dobson. Black, obviously, was the main color with bats, spiders, and creepy crawlies in every shape and form suspended from the ceiling.

Some of the students had made programs that they handed out to any willing audience members as they entered. Unfortunately, they had used black and orange ink cartridges which were not suitable for the school laser printer, so the ink remained wet, and most of the audience took their seats sporting black and orange smudges where their inky hands had touched.

The auditorium was filling up rapidly. Melissa had looked out from behind the heavy curtains earlier and now hurried back to tell her friends they were almost ready to begin. Her heavy black costume prevented her from running too quickly, and her path was obstructed by the odd toad or fairy practicing their lines.

Almost everyone else was in the makeup department (Miss Dobson's office just off-stage).

Melissa reached her two friends. All three were nervous. They had only managed to have one quick run-through of the revised lines after school that day.

Melissa smiled encouragingly at the other two and grabbed their hands. "We'll be just fine," she said reassuringly. "We can do this, you'll see."

The sound of music from the auditorium stopped her from saying more. Miss Dobson had worked with Mr. Rankin, the music teacher, and he had put together a tape of spooky music to give some atmosphere to the play. The opening strains filled the room, then died away to allow the principal to speak.

Mr. Perrie welcomed everyone to the auditorium and as promised, kept his speech as short as possible. The play was introduced and before they knew it, the curtains were back and the girls were on stage!

"This one's for you, Geraldine," whispered Melissa, as she took her position.

CHAPTER THIRTEEN

Showtime

The play opened with the scene in which the three witches chop off Jonathan's finger. Silence fell over the auditorium and Miss Dobson noted, with some satisfaction, that the audience seemed to hang on every word. There were audible gasps when the boy's finger was severed and lots of loud boos as the witches performed their evil tricks. The curtains had been drawn over the windows, which ran from ceiling to floor on one side of the auditorium, so that besides the stage lights, it was almost completely dark. The spooky music provided by Mr. Rankin had been a burst of inspiration. Miss Dobson congratulated herself.

The atmosphere in the auditorium was electric. She turned her attention back to the stage where the raising of the dead scene was being performed. She listened as Jenny repeated her lines.

"He grows warm. Let us complete our task."

Then, as the witches clasped the palms of their hands together, they began to recite the incantation.

"From cold and dark you once did rise. More time on Earth, that was your prize. But no more evil, no black spells. Pray from us go back to where you dwell!"

Miss Dobson looked quizzically at the three girls then searched underneath her chair for her copy of the script. Although parts of what they had said seemed familiar, there was something about it that didn't seem quite right. She thumbed through her dog-eared copy, causing the parents behind her to scowl at her as she rustled through her papers and quickly found the part she was looking for.

"But no more evil," that was what they said,

wasn't it? And she was sure they should have said, "To spread more evil, cast black spells."

She glanced quickly at the faces of the audience members closest to her. No one had noticed. And of course, they wouldn't, she reassured herself, not unless they were familiar with the script like she was. Just when she had thought everything was going to be all right, she thought wryly. She had been so happy to see Melissa, Jo, and Jenny at school earlier that day, and they had assured her they had fully recovered and wouldn't let her down this evening. And now they were getting their lines wrong!

A ripple of laughter echoed through the audience at the antics of one of the trolls who had come on stage. Miss Dobson relaxed. It really didn't matter that one of the incantations had been mixed up— she would put the script back under her chair and just enjoy the rest of the evening. It was funny that all three of the girls had managed to get it wrong though.

Jenny's mom seemed to be the first person to notice the change in temperature. As is usual at functions of this size, rooms filled to capacity with people wearing winter coats, hats, and boots tended to be warm. Not tonight. Jenny's mother soon realized that she was shivering from the cold and reached for the coat she had discarded earlier to wrap around her shoulders. One by one, most of the people in the audience did the same thing, donning scarves and gloves as Mr. Perrie got up and walked over to check whether or not the heat was on.

The radiator was ice cold. He whispered to Mr. Rankin and left the auditorium to speak to the janitor. Even the students on stage began to be aware of the icy cold filling the auditorium.

Melissa and her two friends exchanged glances.

"I think it's working," whispered Melissa as she stamped her feet in a vain attempt to get warm. "The witches are upset. We have to keep it up!"

Mr. Perrie returned to the auditorium. He had

been unable to find the janitor, and he himself had no knowledge of how of the heating system worked. As the door closed behind him, a blanket of warm air followed him into the room. He touched the radiator as he passed and was amazed to find that it was now warm.

Mr. Rankin smiled and gave him the thumbs up sign, and he smiled back. He hadn't actually done anything to solve the problem of the cold, but Mr. Rankin didn't need to know that, did he?

It's Geraldine, Melissa thought as the warm air reached her. She's fighting back. She smiled and crossed her fingers as she continued with the play.

Acts Two and Three passed more or less uneventfully; although, Miss Dobson noticed the girls get some more of the lines wrong. Nothing major and nothing anyone else would pick up on, but maybe the last line of a spell would be incorrect or a whole chant would be recited in the wrong order. It really was strange. After all, it was only meant to be Jenny who had suffered the concussion.

The next and final act, Act Four, started off fine. It was the one that showed the witches conjure up all the powers of evil in order to help them banish good from the earth. The three girls knew this was the important one, the one they could not afford to get wrong, or right to be more accurate.

When the curtains opened, the huge, steaming cauldron had been placed center stage and the three witches stood beside it. The trolls and hobgoblins, their helpers, danced around the stage, alternately grimacing and shouting at the audience. The witches stood behind the cauldron and stared out at the sea of expectant faces. The spell book had been placed on a podium to the right and Melissa took her place beside it and began to read.

"In order for this spell to work properly," she began in a croaky voice, "it is important that only the freshest ingredients are used."

She began to read out the list.

"One: the forked tongue of a living serpent. Two: the fluffy tail of a white rabbit, which has been dipped in the still-warm blood of a sixth grader."

All the sixth graders slunk lower into their seats. Miss Dobson scrambled for her script, but as she did so, the doors of the hall started to bang open and shut, open and shut, open and shut, and icy blasts of air blew her script out of her grasp. The girls on stage had to raise their voices so they could be heard over the banging of the doors.

"Three," called Melissa loudly, this time aided by Jo and Jenny. "The brain of a principal, to be boiled in the cauldron before being removed and eaten, slowly."

This was utter nonsense, thought Miss Dobson, rising to her feet. She was forced back into her seat when all the windows blew wide open and flocks of crows flew into the auditorium, squawking loudly as they flew over the heads of the audience, adding to the general mayhem.

Mr. Perrie was unexpectedly enjoying himself. These performances usually turned out to be tedious affairs, and on more than one occasion in the past, he had found himself nodding off to sleep. But not tonight! The acting and props had been excellent and the special effects were something else. He had to ask Miss Dobson later about how she managed to get the crows to fly in the windows. That really was creative.

Melissa, Jo, and Jenny were shouting now.

"Four: two large rats, one black and one brown, and a box full of squirming white maggots."

There was a screech on stage and Miss Dobson looked up to see that a fourth witch had joined the girls on stage. Who on earth was she? She peered at the witch's face but failed to recognize her.

"No!" the fourth witch screamed, outraged. "That's not what you're supposed to say. Those are not the lines that were written for you. The lines you're meant to be reading are, 'One: cabbage and caterpillars with compressed spiders' webs. Two: bat's blood mixed with deadly nightshade. Three: foxglove juice and boar's grease.' And, lastly," she screeched, as her two sisters joined her on stage, "'four: the pure, gold heart of a pretty, young girl.'"

The audience was entranced. There were six witches on stage now, crows flying all around the auditorium, and the doors were still banging open and shut. They couldn't wait to see what would happen next.

The smallest girl on stage, Mary, had tried to leave with the rest of the trolls when the three older witches appeared, but she had been too slow. The witch closest to her grabbed the girl and tucked her under her arm. The girl screamed loudly as the witch carrying her began making her way toward the cauldron in the center of the stage.

"Leave her alone," called Melissa. "Your time on Earth is over! Go back to where you belong."

The witch laughed in response.

"It's not over yet, my dear. Look! We have the child. A child who possesses a pure, gold heart—we merely need to find the rest of the ingredients and our reign here will continue for as long as we want."

But the witch was growing weak and knew her steps faltered as she toiled with the weight of the little girl. She knelt on the floor.

"Quickly, sister," she said, "help me, before we lose any more strength. You must open the child and remove her heart so that we may place it in the cauldron."

The witch pushed back the sleeve of her cloak, revealing the sharp knife-like objects that served as her fingers.

Suddenly, a light flickered on in the auditorium and some words were projected onto a screen. Leading the way, Melissa, Jo, and Jenny began to chant the words, and were soon joined by the audience.

"Everything that's rotting here, we tell you to go. Go and join the evil in the darkness down below. Take your cauldrons and your tricks to the world below the floor! Go from us where you belong! We'll see you nevermore!"

The chant grew louder and louder as the audience repeated it over and over again. The three witches were now so weak that they could only fall on the stage and beg for mercy.

Jenny ran across the stage and grabbed hold of Mary, holding her and telling her that everything would be all right as the girl cried.

Just before the final curtain closed, Mr. Perrie thought, although it could have been a trick of the light, that he saw the three figures disintegrate into three tiny piles of sand.

CHAPTER FOURTEEN

All Is Well...Or Is It?

It was a bright morning that reminded the girls of the promise of summer days to come.

They placed the flowers they had brought with them at the foot of Geraldine Somers's grave. The wind and rain from the previous week had destroyed the flowers that had been there the last time the girls had visited.

The three of them knelt, and Melissa brushed some stray wet petals from the lettering on Geraldine's gravestone.

"She's at peace now, hopefully, and what we did should mean that her rest is never disturbed again," said Melissa.

The girls had, in conjunction with Miss Dobson, destroyed every copy they could find of the play so that it would never be performed again. Even though they hadn't disclosed every detail of the events that had taken place, Miss Dobson had been sufficiently spooked and agreed with them that it would be best if the play was destroyed.

"So?" began Jo as the girls stood up and started to leave. "Are you meeting Jonathan tonight? Not that I'm jealous or anything." She smiled at Melissa.

Melissa and Jonathan getting together had been one of the few good things to come out of the play.

"Yes, I'm going to watch him play basketball and then we're going out to eat." Melissa smiled happily. "What about you two?"

Jo said she was going back for a second shot at ice-skating with her niece.

"I'm determined to conquer this," she laughed. "After all, the scar on my knee is almost gone from the last time."

Both girls looked at Jenny, who smiled shyly.

"I'm going to the hospital," she said, "to visit Danny."

Both her friends looked shocked.

"Danny Cottrill?" asked Melissa.

"Yes, I know, the school bully, but I've been getting to know him over the past week or so since he came out of his coma, and he's actually really nice. I didn't know his parents only moved here right before the school year. He said he was so insecure that he acted the way he did just to get some attention. Unwarranted attention, I should add. Anyway, the doctors say he's going to be all right, no permanent damage, and he should be out of the hospital in a few more weeks."

The three girls walked down the path and out of the cemetery, closing the gate behind them.

"So, there's a happy ending after all," said Melissa as they walked off, heading home.

What the girls didn't see were the pages that

fluttered one by one onto Geraldine Somers's grave. The fresh flowers they had laid were almost obscured from view by the yellowed pages that fell on top of them. When the top page fell, any onlookers who passed would have been able to read these words:

Oh Spirits Obey Us
Written by Geraldine Somers

Read on to enjoy an excerpt from another
haunting title in the Creepers series:

Pen Pals

by Edgar J. Hyde

Illustrations by Chloe Tyler

Chapter One

"Natasha Morris, will you please tell me, and the rest of your classmates, what on earth is so interesting outside?"

With a jolt, Natasha turned toward the teacher.

"I'm sorry, Miss Harrison, I was just thinking about..." Natasha's voice trailed off.

She couldn't think of an excuse, and she couldn't possibly tell the truth—that this morning's long-winded history lesson was boring! After all, wasn't history supposed to be about Henry VIII and his six wives, romance, divorce, and gory beheadings? Instead she was having to sit and listen for two hours about crop rotation! Crop rotation—who on earth cared?

"No. Don't even bother stuttering your way through an excuse, just do me a favor and pay attention. Remember you have a test coming up next week, and crop rotation just might be one of the questions!" Miss Harrison turned to the rest of the class. "Now, where were we?" Her voice droned on and on.

Olivia turned and smiled at Natasha sympathetically. The two were best friends and had been since they first met up as four-year-olds in the same preschool. They were now in their first year of high school, enjoying feeling grown-up, carrying their books from class to class around the massive, never-ending hallways, giggling as they frequently got lost, only to arrive red and breathless to their next class. They had made new friends, too.

There was Ellis, with her dark curly hair and large brown eyes. Natasha envied her. Then there was Marcie, though Natasha couldn't make up her mind about her just yet. She was the complete opposite of Ellis, pale with long, straw-like blonde hair and somewhat on the quiet side. Pale and interesting, I guess, if you were being nice, thought Natasha.

She hastily scribbled a note and passed it to Olivia without Miss Harrison noticing.

Meet you outside the library at four.

Olivia quickly pushed the note inside her notebook and gave no sign of having received anything.

Natasha looked at her watch. Ten minutes past four. Where on earth was Olivia? Just then, she saw Olivia, Marcie, and Ellis wind their way up the long path from the front of the school.

"You took your time." She smiled as all three girls stopped just beside her.

"Sorry, Natasha, it's my fault," said Ellis. "I left

my new lip gloss in the bathroom and had to go get it. You never know who you might see on the way home."

Ellis was always experimenting with lip gloss and eye shadow and always on the lookout for free samples. She would come to school drenched in perfume, having spent the weekend in the perfume department of the nearest store.

"You should try some, Marcie. Look, it's a pale pink, it'd look great on you."

"Gosh, no," said Marcie. "My mom would freak out. She says there's plenty of time to put all that 'junk,' as she calls it, on my face. Anyway, I'd rather keep my money for important things. I'm going to buy some new headphones this weekend, at least they will last longer than your makeup will!"

"Hey, Ellis," someone shouted from behind them. The girls turned to see Scott Gregson across from them. He was the best looking guy in their grade, and everyone had their eye on him. "If you're going home, I'll walk with you."

Ellis smiled. "See what the 'junk' on your face does for you, girls," she muttered. "Sure, Scott, I was just saying goodbye to the girls. See you tomorrow, everybody." And off she went, pink lips glistening, dark curls bouncing, backpack slung casually over her arm.

"Don't you just wish you had her confidence," sighed Olivia.

"Yes, and her hair and her teeth and her eyes," replied Natasha. "Never mind, 'Make the best of what you've got' is what my mom always says. Now let's see, what could you make out of the three of us?"

And as the three started to make their way home, they laughed together, picking out the parts of each other that they thought were the "best."

"Okay, Natasha," said Olivia, "you give me your tiny waist, Marcie can give me her small perfectly shaped feet, and I can probably get away with using my own hands—if I paint my fingernails—and with the help of a wig, there we have it, the perfect girl!"

And so the conversation carried on until the girls were almost home.

"Oh, and Natasha," Olivia began, "next time you write me a note in class, you really don't have to write my full name on it. I know who I am!"

Natasha looked at Olivia. "I didn't write your full name, Olivia. In fact, I didn't even write your first name!"

"Yes, you did," Olivia laughed, as she fished in both jacket pockets for the note. "You wrote, 'Olivia Goulden, meet you outside the library at four.' Darn, I can't find the note—oh, look, here it is."

They had now reached Marcie's house and Olivia had emptied the contents of her backpack onto the pavement outside. She showed the hastily scrawled note to Natasha and sure enough, Olivia's name was written above what Natasha remembered writing.

Olivia Goulden,
Meet you outside the library at four.

"That's really weird, Olivia. I don't remember writing that, it doesn't even look like my handwriting."

"Marcie, where have you been?" the girls heard Marcie's mom shout from an upstairs window.

"Oops, gotta go! Mom wants me to go to the grocery store with her today. See you tomorrow."

"Bye, Marcie," called the two girls as she disappeared inside her front door.

Natasha was still staring at the note.

"Stop trying to be funny, Natasha. I mean if you passed the note straight to me and I didn't add my own name to it, then who did?" Olivia protested. "Anyway, look, I have to run too. I'm babysitting Mrs. Winter's twins tonight, and I have to try and get my homework done before I go. I'll see you tomorrow."

"All right," sighed Natasha, "but I still don't understand."

She left Olivia at the end of the street where the road leading to her house forked left.

Weird, she thought as she walked, she must have been in more of a bored stupor than she realized this morning. How could you write someone's name and not remember?

"Suzanna Craigson," she read aloud from one of the gravestones in the cemetery. She had to pass the cemetery every morning and afternoon going to and from school, and although she was never comfortable with it, she found the best way around it was to make up stories about the people lying beneath the rows and rows of tombstones. That way it took the scariness out of it.

"Born November 2, 1806. Cruelly taken from her beloved parents November 1, 1820."

Natasha had never noticed that particular stone before, or maybe it was just that she had never

Suzanna
Craigson

Born November 2, 1806
cruelly taken from
her beloved parents
November 1, 1820

actually realized how young Suzanna had been when she died.

Wonder what happened to her, she thought. The use of the word "cruelly" seemed to indicate murder or something gory and horrible.

Better stop thinking about it, she decided. Mom always says my imagination's too vivid. It'll end up getting me into trouble one of these days.

"Here comes fatso, here comes fatso." Her young brother's chanting soon stopped her daydreaming.

"Come here, Tommy, you little brat," she laughed, chasing the bubbly little three-year-old into the backyard. "I'll show you fatso."

She grabbed him and hugged him tightly around the waist, lifting him right off his feet. She kissed him loudly on the lips and came away covered in green sticky goo.

"What have you been eating now?" She smiled.

"Gooey monsters," he said and showed her the

empty packet.

"Green Slimy Guts," she read aloud. "Made from jelly and packets of sugar and full of additives." She added, "Your teeth will fall out," and poked him in the tummy playfully.

"Don't care about teef," he retorted. "Like gooey monsters!"

How did the rhyme go, she mused as she went inside to change. Sugar and spice and all things nice, oh yes, frogs and snails and puppy dogs' tails, or something like that. Tommy was that, all right, and she adored every last little inch of him. She wondered if Suzanna Craigson had had a brother.

Pen Pals

ISBN: 9781486718757
Available: November 3, 2020

The Scarecrow

ISBN: 9781486718788
Available: October 6, 2020

Stage Fright

ISBN: 9781486718771
Available: September 1, 2020